Alice Goes to Hollywood

by Karen Wallace
illustrated by Bob Dewar

PICTURE WINDOW BOOKS
Minneapolis, Minnesota

To Susila, who knows about anteaters—KW

Editor: Jill Kalz
Page Production: Melissa Kes
Creative Director: Keith Griffin
Editorial Director: Carol Jones

First American edition published in 2006 by
Picture Window Books
5115 Excelsior Boulevard
Suite 232
Minneapolis, MN 55416
877-845-8392
www.picturewindowbooks.com

First published in Great Britain by
A & C Black Publishers Ltd
37 Soho Square, London, W1D 3QZ
www.acblack.com
Text copyright © 2005 Karen Wallace
Illustrations copyright © 2005 Bob Dewar

Printed in the United States of America.

Library of Congress Cataloging-in-Publication Data
Wallace, Karen.
Alice goes to Hollywood / written by Karen Wallace ; illustrated by Bob Dewar.
p. cm. — (Read-it! chapter books)
Summary: Alice the anteater leaves the jungle to pursue her dream of becoming a film
star in Hollywood.
ISBN 1-4048-1678-X (hardcover)
[1. Anteaters—Fiction. 2. Jungles—Fiction. 3. Hollywood (Los Angeles, Calif.)—Fiction.]
I. Dewar, Bob, ill. II. Title. III. Series.
PZ7.W1568Ali 2005
[Fic]—dc22   2005030013

Table of Contents

Chapter One 5

Chapter Two 15

Chapter Three 24

Chapter Four 33

Chapter Five 41

Chapter Six 46

Chapter One

Alice was an anteater who lived in the jungle.

Every day, she dug for ants with her sharp, curved claws. Then she slurped them up with her long, curling tongue.

When Alice was full, she curled up in a ball and snoozed in the sunshine.

Alice was an anteater. Eating ants and snoozing is what anteaters do.

One day, Alice found a magazine stuck on a thorn bush. It was called *Fabulous Movie Stars*. It was all about famous people and the amazing movies they made.

Alice made a big decision. "I am going to be a movie star!" she told the other anteaters. "Just you wait and see."

"Don't be silly, Alice," said the other anteaters. "You're an anteater!"

"Eat up your ants," said her mother at supper time. "They're your favorite."

Alice turned up her snout. "Movie stars don't eat ants," she said. "Ants are tickly, prickly, *yucky* things!"

Days passed. While the other anteaters went to dig up ants, Alice stayed at home and taught herself to tap dance.

While the other anteaters snoozed in the trees, Alice taught herself to sing.

And when she was alone in the jungle,
Alice practiced speaking in different voices.

One afternoon, while the other anteaters were digging for ants, Alice painted her toenails purple and her lips pink. Then she went to see Cornelius the Crocodile.

Chapter Two

Cornelius was lying in the water. When he saw Alice, he waddled onto the shore.

Cornelius loved visitors because he loved talking. But sadly, Cornelius didn't get many visitors because sometimes he forgot his manners and gobbled them up.

Alice stood far away from Cornelius. She looked at his sharp teeth. "Hello," she said nervously. "How are you?"

"Completely full," replied Cornelius. He yawned. His mouth was as big as a cave. "I heard you want to be a movie star."

"I *will* be a movie star," said Alice.

"I once ate a movie star," said
Cornelius. "Would you like to hear the
whole story?"

"No, thank you," said Alice quickly.
She knew that once Cornelius started talking,
it was almost impossible to make him stop.

"How can I help?" asked Cornelius.

"I need clothes to go to Hollywood," said Alice.

"Then you must look in my dress-up box," replied Cornelius. "It's full of things that I've … uh … collected."

Cornelius ran his tongue along his teeth and waddled back into the water. Alice found the dress-up box and opened it. She had never seen so many wonderful things!

Alice chose a blue scarf, a pair of high-heeled sandals, a frilly dress, a purse shaped like a heart, and a long, blond wig.

She put them on and stared at her reflection in the water. It was amazing. She looked just like a movie star! There was just one thing missing.

Alice looked in the dress-up box again and found what she wanted—a pair of movie-star sunglasses! "Yes!" she cried, punching the air.

Then, without saying good-bye to anyone, Alice paddled down the river and took the first plane to Hollywood.

to the
Airport

Chapter Three

Alice *loved* Hollywood! She loved the
flashing signs, the fast cars, and the big,
fancy hotels.

Most of all, Alice loved the movie stars. They crowded around her every day, saying, "Gee! Aren't you cute?"

Men with huge cameras followed Alice wherever she went. Soon her picture was in all of the magazines.

Alice was delighted. "I'm famous!" she cried. "I'm a movie star at last!"

She cut out her photograph and sent it home to the jungle.

See! I did it!

Love
xxx
Alice.
(movie)
(Star)

Mom and everyone.
The Jungle
FaraWay

There was only one problem.

Alice knew she had to be in a movie if she wanted to be a *real* movie star. But every time she talked about finding a job, the movie stars asked her the same two questions: "Is it true you live in the jungle?" "What's it like eating ants?"

One day, Alice met an important movie director. He was thin with shiny eyes. He looked like a snake.

"I want to be a movie star!" said Alice.

"But you're an anteater," said the director.

"An anteater can be a movie star!" said Alice.

Alice showed him all of the things she had taught herself to do. She danced ...

... and sang ...

Do, Re, Mi, Fa, So, La, Ti, Do!

... and spoke in different voices.

"Whaddyathink?" asked Alice in her
best Hollywood accent.

The director shrugged. "Don't call me, I'll call you," he said.

"What does that mean?" asked Alice.

"It means that I don't have any parts for anteaters," said the director.

Chapter Four

That night, Alice went to a big, fancy party.
The room was packed with movie stars.

Cameras clicked. Flashbulbs popped. All of the movie stars wanted to have their picture taken with Alice. "Gee!" they cried. "A real live anteater! Is it true you live in the jungle and eat ants?"

Poor Alice! No matter what she said, they didn't listen. They didn't believe an anteater could be a movie star.

Alice tiptoed outside and sat in the shadows. Two movie stars walked onto the balcony.

"Did you hear that anteater?" asked one.

"Silly animal," said the other. "She thinks she's going to be a movie star."

They laughed and went back inside.

Alice crawled under a bush where no one could see her. Tears poured down her wrinkly snout. She thought of the other anteaters hunting happily in the jungle, and she felt very, very lonely.

"Don't cry, Alice," squeaked a voice.
A hedgehog was standing beside her. "I saw
your picture in the paper," he whispered.
"I've always wanted to meet an anteater."

The hedgehog blinked shyly and held out a gold box. "This is for you," he said.

Alice opened the box slowly. It was full of munchy, crunchy ants.

For the first time since she had arrived in Hollywood, Alice felt really hungry.

Alice slurped up the ants with her long, curling tongue. It was as if some kind of spell was broken. Suddenly, she knew exactly what she should do!

Chapter Five

Alice pulled off her long, blond wig and ripped her frilly dress in two.

She took off her high-heeled sandals
and threw them away ...

... and stomped on her movie-star sunglasses.

She was about to throw her purse away, but then she decided not to. After all, even an anteater needs a purse sometimes.

"What are you doing?" asked the puzzled hedgehog.

"I'm going home!" cried Alice happily. "As soon as I tasted those ants, I knew I was never meant to be a movie star. I'm an anteater, through and through!"

Alice hugged the hedgehog. "Thanks, buddy," she said in a perfect Hollywood accent. "You've done me a big favor." And she planted a kiss on his prickly nose.

The hedgehog trembled all over. It was his dream to be kissed by an anteater. "Come with me," he said. "I'll show you the way to the airport."

Chapter Six

The next day, back at home, Alice found
Cornelius lying in the water. When he saw
Alice, he waddled onto the shore.

"So, how was Hollywood?" he asked.
"What were the movie stars like?"

Alice made a face. "Hollywood was horrible, and the movie stars were rude."

Cornelius blinked his big, yellow eyes. "If you hadn't been in such a hurry," he said, "I could have warned you."

"How do *you* know?" asked Alice.

"They don't taste good," said Cornelius. He yawned. "It's usually a bad sign."

All of the other anteaters were delighted to see Alice. Her mother gave her an extra-big hug.

"Welcome home!" she cried. "We've been waiting for you!"

She gave Alice a special supper. There were ants in everything!

Welcome Home, Alice

MOM's MENU

Ant Soup
Ant Pie
Ant Jelly

Later, when everyone was asleep, Alice watched the moon rise. It shone on the jungle and made it look silver. She turned over and snuggled into her pile of leaves.

For the first time in ages, Alice was completely happy. And she dreamed about ants all night long!

Look for More
Read-it!
Chapter Books

Bricks for Breakfast 1-4048-1275-X

Buffalo Bert: The Cowboy Grandad 1-4048-1660-7

Detective Dan 1-4048-1659-3

Duncan and the Pirates 1-4048-1277-6

Hetty the Yeti 1-4048-1276-8

The Mean Team from Mars 1-4048-1274-1

Milo in a Mess 1-4048-1679-8

Spookball Champions 1-4048-1278-4

Toby and His Old Tin Tub 1-4048-1279-2

Treasure at the Flea Market 1-4048-1661-5

Looking for a specific title? A complete list of *Read-it!* Chapter Books is available on our Web site: **www.picturewindowbooks.com**